My 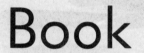 Book

by Jane Belk Moncure

illustrated by Linda Hohag

THE CHILD'S WORLD

ELGIN, ILLINOIS 60120

Library of Congress Cataloging in Publication Data

Moncure, Jane Belk.
  My "s" book.

  (My first steps to reading)
  Rev. ed. of: My s sound box. © 1977.
  Summary: Little s goes for a walk along the sea
and finds many things that begin with the letter "s"
to put in his box.
  1. Children's stories, American.   [1. Alphabet]
I. Hohag, Linda. ill.   II. Moncure, Jane Belk.   My
s sound box.   III. Title.   IV. Series: Moncure, Jane
Belk.   My first steps to reading.
PZ7.M739Mys   1984   [E]   84-17551
ISBN 0-89565-291-9

Distributed by Childrens Press, 1224 West Van Buren Street,
Chicago, Illinois 60607.

My "s" Book

(The "sh" sound is included in this book along with blends.)

Little  S had a  box.

He said, "I will fill my  box."

Little  S took off his

shoes,

socks,

sweater,

and shirt.

He put them into his box.

Little S put on his swimsuit and his sandals.

Then he went for a walk.

9

He found  a shovel,
a sand pail,
and a sand castle.

He put them into his box.

Little S went for a swim.

He saw a seal swimming
in the sea.

He saw six seals on the sand.
Did he put them into his box?

He did!

Little s found
seashells,
lots of seashells.

14

He found a

starfish too.

"In you go," he said.

box

Then he saw a
shark.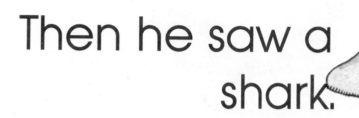

He put the shark into
a sack.

He put the sack
into his box.

Little  saw a sea snake.

He put the sea snake
into a sack too.
Do you know why?

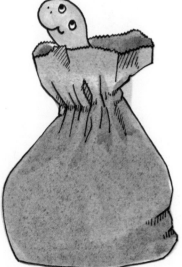

Later Little  S met a sailor.

"Hi," he said.

Guess what the sailor gave him?
A sailor hat.

"You can be a sailor," he said.

They played on
the see-saw.

They slid down the

slide.

They swang in the swings.

Suddenly they heard a loud sound.

"What is in your box?" asked the sailor.

"Things that begin  with my sound," said Little S.

"I sail on things that begin with your sound," said the sailor.

"I sail on a ship.

"I sail on a  submarine."

Guess what Little  S said?
"I want to sail."

Little S took

along

his box.

slide

sailor

sho

seven seals

swing

sandals

shovel

sand
pail

sand castle

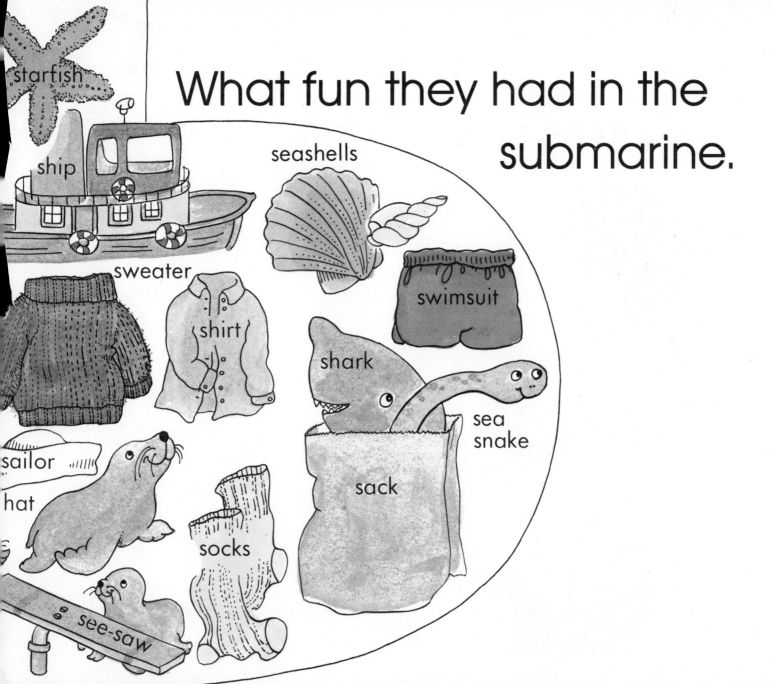

What fun they had in the submarine.

starfish

ship

seashells

sweater

shirt

swimsuit

shark

sea snake

sailor hat

sack

socks

see-saw

27

More words with Little .

sunflower

stick

snail

sink

soap

star

salad

seed

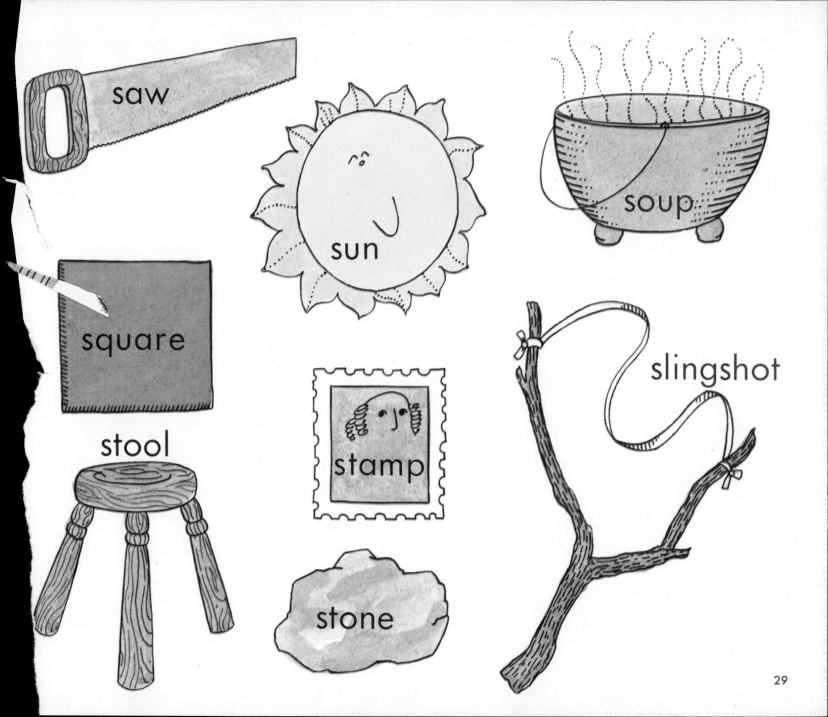

saw

sun

soup

square

slingshot

stool

stamp

stone

29